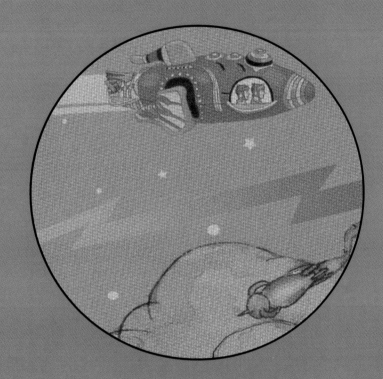

I Want to Go to the Moon

For my wonderful family and friends, and especially
Dan, Chloe, Sue and Liz! - Tom

For Ralph (King of the ukulele) Shaw, who made
everything possible. - Cynthia

Published in 2011 by Simply Read Books www.simplyreadbooks.com
Text © 2011 Tom Saunders Illustrations © 2011 Cynthia Nugent
All rights reserved. No part of this publication may be reproduced,
stored in a retrieval system, or transmitted, in any form or by any
means, electronic, mechanical, photocopying, recording or otherwise,
without the written permission of the publisher. The publisher
does not have any control over and does not assume any
responsibility for author or third-party websites or their content.

We gratefully acknowledge for their financial support of our
publishing program the Canada Council for the Arts, the BC
Arts Council, and the Government of Canada through the Book
Publishing Industry Development Program (BPIDP).

Book design by Elisa Gutiérrez
Interior text set in Jopa and Handegypt. Both © MADType

Manufactured in China   10 9 8 7 6 5 4 3 2 1

LIBRARY AND ARCHIVES CANADA CATALOGUING IN PUBLICATION

Saunders, Tom, 1958-
   I want to go to the moon / written by Tom Saunders ; illustrated by
Cynthia Nugent.

Based on lyrics of author's song with same title.
Accompanied by a CD.
ISBN 978-1-897476-56-7

   1. Armstrong, Neil, 1930- --Juvenile poetry. 2. Space flight to the
moon--Juvenile poetry. 3. Project Apollo (U.S.)--Juvenile poetry.
4. Children's poetry, Canadian (English). I. Nugent, Cynthia, 1954-
II. Title.

PS8637.A798I17 2010   jC811'.6   C2010-904529-7

I Want to Go to the Moon

words and music by
Tom Saunders

pictures by
Cynthia Nugent

Simply Read Books

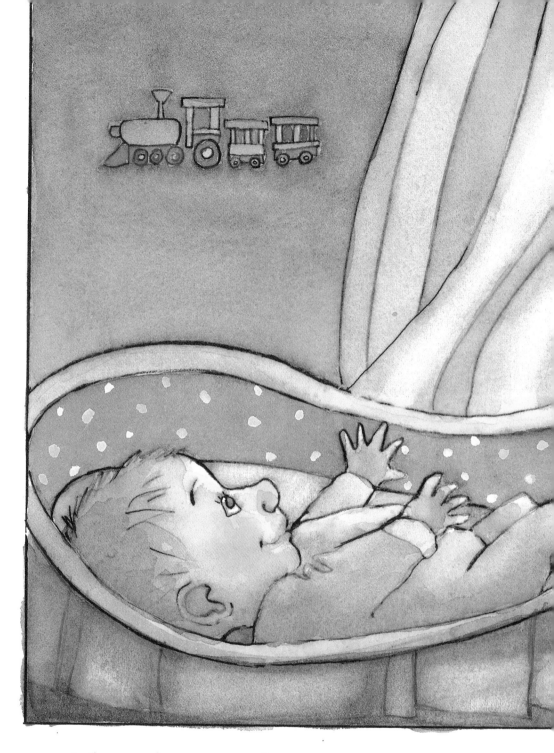

Neil was born one August morn,
not a day too soon,

and every night he pointed
out his window at the moon.

When he took his first small steps
and said his first few words,
he marched up to his parents' room,
and this is what they heard:

"I want to go to the moon, Mom.
I want to go to the moon, Dad.
What can I do to make it come true?
I want to go to the moon."

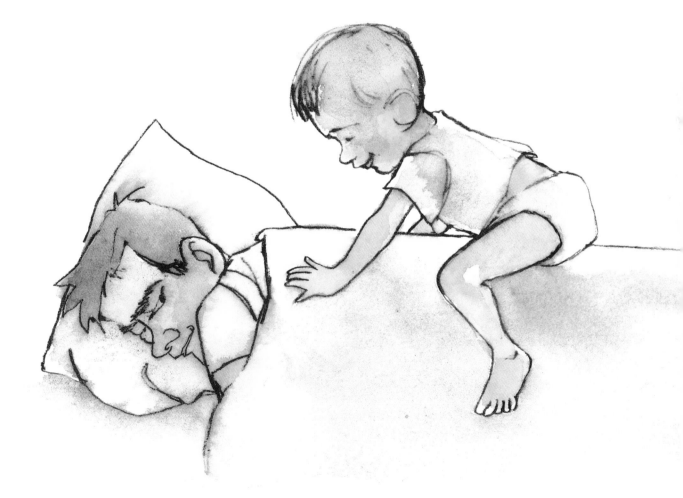

His parents loved him very much
and tried to make him see
the spaceships in the storybooks
were only make-believe.

"You see, my son, it's not been long
since man began to fly.
The moon's too far away
and that's why no one's even tried."

"You'll never go to the moon, Neil.
You'll never go to the moon.
We're sorry, my son,
but it's never been done.
You'll never go to the moon."

He built himself a rocket ship
the day that he turned six.
The other kids ate birthday cake,
while Neil worked on the ship.
Everyone in his neighborhood
thought his rocket ship was good.
But they all squealed when Neil revealed,
"I'm going there for real."

"You'll never go to the moon, Neil.
You'll never go to the moon,
You silly young Neilly, it isn't for really.
You'll never go to the moon."

Neil went to school and studied hard
morning, night and noon.
Just so he could be prepared
to walk upon the moon.
His teachers told him not to waste
his time on crazy dreams.
"It's good to have a goal," they said,
"but yours is too extreme."

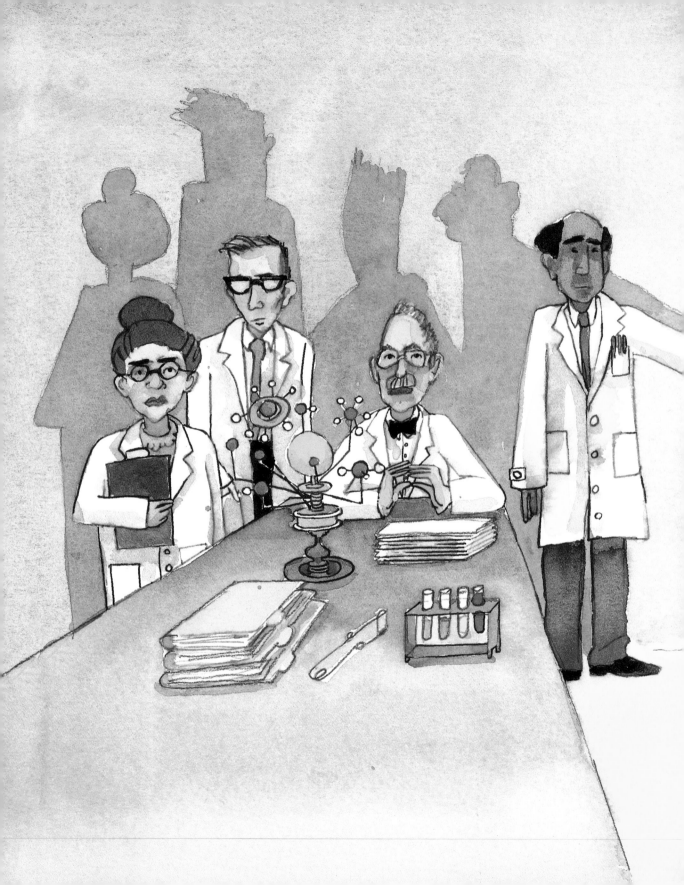

"You'll never go to the moon, Neil.
You'll never go to the moon.
Scientists say that it's too far away.
You'll never go to the moon."

And when he finished college,
with his suitcase in his car,
he drove to where they built the rockets
headed to the stars.
They said, "The only job we have
is cleaning knives and spoons."
Neil said, "Okay, I'll do it, but –
I want to go to the moon."

"No, you'll never go to the moon, Neil.
You'll never go to the moon.
You're the back of the line
of a million and nine.
You'll never go to the moon."

yeeha!

yippee!

oops!

Neil washed the spoons at night,
and in the day he trained to fly
the highest, fastest planes
that ever flew up in the sky.
He earned his wings by flying up
the highest in a jet.
But Neil said, "Till I reach the moon
- we ain't seen nothing yet."

"Oh, you'll never go to the moon, Neil.
You'll never go to the moon.
That's the way that it goes, and everyone knows,
you'll never go to the moon."

Neil was made an astronaut in 1962.
The finest of the finest made
the first Apollo crew.
And then in 1969, one summer afternoon,
the General said, "We need someone
to take us to the moon."

"Do you wanna go to the moon, Neil?
Do you wanna go to the moon?
You've proven yourself, like nobody else.
You're gonna go to the moon."

Three, two, one - LIFT OFF!

"Oh, you made it to the moon, Neil.
You made it to the moon.
You did what you said and
you said what you did,
and you made it to the moon."